King Jayko
© 2006 LEGO

Sir Kentis
© 2006 LEGO

Lord Vladek
© 2006 LEGO

Sir Adric
© 2006 LEGO

Karzon
© 2006 LEGO

Dracus
© 2006 LEGO

The Magic of the Tower

By Michael Anthony Steele
Illustrated by Mike Rayhawk

SCHOLASTIC INC.

New York   Toronto   London   Auckland   Sydney
Mexico City   New Delhi   Hong Kong   Buenos Aires

ISBN 0-439-82812-0

12 11 10 9 8 7 6 5 4 3 2   7 8 9 10/0

Printed in the U.S.A.
First printing, November 2006

After a dangerous journey, King Jayko and his knights finally reached Gargoyle Bridge. They planned to use the tower's forge to repair the shattered Shield of Ages. But the evil Lord Vladek wanted the tower's magic for himself and he was not far behind.

"Look, my king!" shouted Sir Kentis.

A mighty battering ram rumbled toward them. Riding atop was Karzon, one of Vladek's Rogue Knights.

"I'll stop that Rogue!" declared Sir Adric. His red armor streaked as he bounded up the steps to where two giant battle-axes hung.

Using his own battle-axe, Adric chopped through the chains that held the huge axes. The enormous weapons slammed against the stone bridge. The structure crumbled, and both Karzon and his battering ram fell to the murky water below.

SPLASH!

Now that the bridge had been destroyed, the Rogue Knights would have to find another way into the Mistlands Tower.

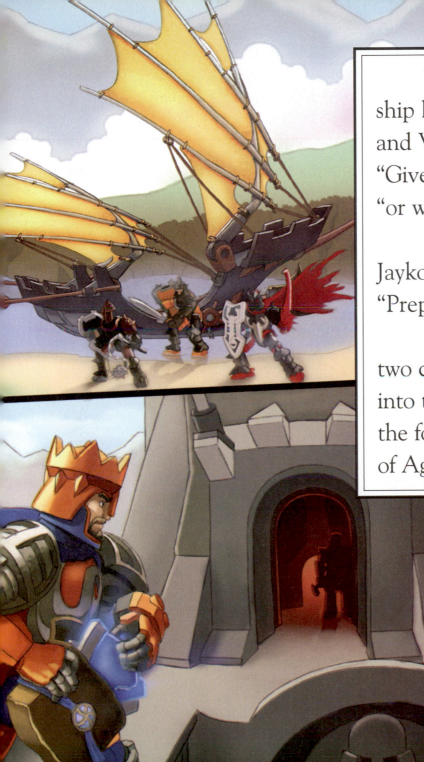

The Rogue Knight battleship landed at the front gate and Vladek stepped ashore. "Give up the tower," he ordered, "or we'll take it by force!"

"Never!" shouted King Jayko. He turned to his knights. "Prepare to attack!"

Kentis and Adric loaded two catapults as the king darted into the tower. He had to find the forge and repair the Shield of Ages!

King Jayko discovered the forge but was surprised to find a mysterious blacksmith hard at work beside the roaring fire. The king removed the shattered Shield of Ages from his pouch.

"Could it be?" The blacksmith's eyes widened. He quickly took the pieces of the broken shield and began to repair it.

On the shore, Vladek repelled the knights' catapult attacks. Lightning erupted from his sword and blasted the boulders from the sky.

"If only I had the materials to build a mighty weapon," Vladek growled.

"There, my lord!" Dracus, one of Vladek's Rogue Knights, pointed at the remains of an ancient battlement.

"Perfect!" Vladek smiled and aimed his sword at the rubble.

Using dark magic, Vladek raised the debris in the air and formed a menacing weapon. "Jayko and his men will be no match for this!" Vladek said, pleased.

Dracus aimed the weapon at the main gate. Instead of firing stones, the ballista fired a bolt. Half of the tower gate exploded.

Vladek quickly created a second catapult that launched jagged saw blades.

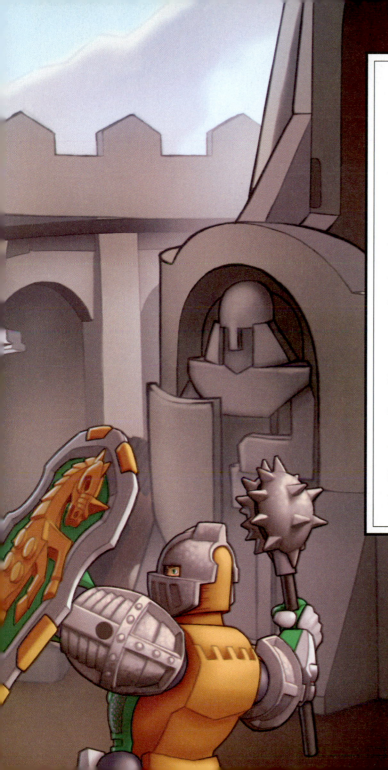

BAM! Sir Kentis and Sir Adric raised their shields as the rest of the gate was blown off.

"Kentis, we must retreat," Adric called as both men dodged spinning saw blades.

Vladek and his knights saw their chance and charged. *KLINK, KLANK, KLINK!* Weapons struck shields as the fierce warriors battled each other.

During the battle, the knights cleverly backed Dracus and Karzon over a large trapdoor.

"Take that, you Rogues!" Kentis called as he sprung the trap. The Rogue Knights fell to the dungeon below. Adric jumped away just in time.

But Vladek slipped through and ran to the top of the tower. Carrying the repaired Shield of Ages, King Jayko followed. He reached the top just as Vladek smashed the magical blue orb.

Waves of energy washed over Vladek. "Now I am invincible!"

King Jayko raised the shield as Vladek blasted him with fire.

Once Adric and Kentis reached the top of the tower they pressed their shields against the king's. All three shields began to glow. "This is the Shield of Ages," the king announced. "Whoever holds it can defeat any enemy!"

A wave of blue energy surrounded Vladek. "Nooooo!"

To their surprise, when the king and his knights lowered their shields, the orb was whole again . . . and Vladek was trapped inside.

Their enemy defeated, King Jayko and his knights returned to Morcia. There, the king made Sir Adric and Sir Kentis part of the Royal Order of the King's Knights. Both had proven to be true Knights of Morcia!

Back at his castle, King Jayko gazed out over his peaceful kingdom.

Jayko looked up at the statue of Orlan, first Knight of Morcia. To his surprise, he recognized the stone face. It looked a lot like the mysterious blacksmith in the Mistlands Tower. King Jayko smiled.

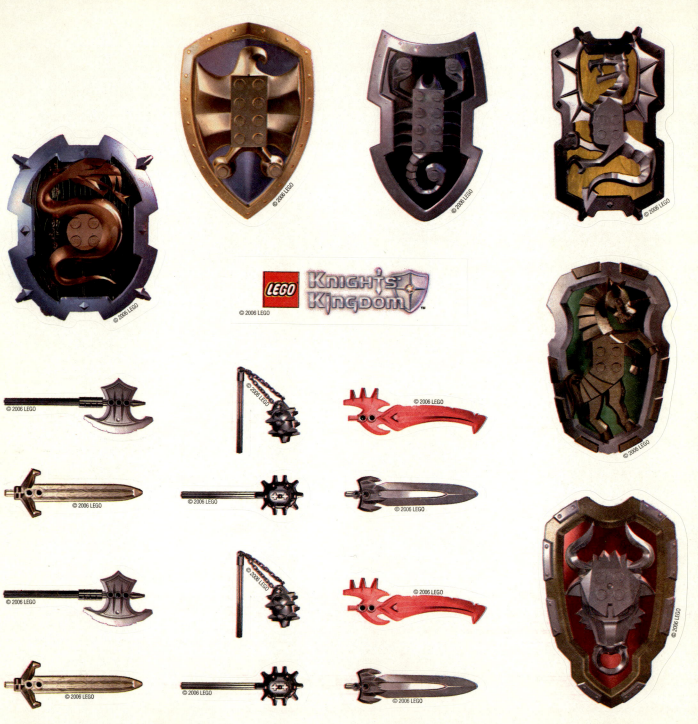

© 2006 LEGO

KNIGHTS' KINGDOM

© 2006 LEGO